CRITS OF PENGUIN

A CAT CALLED PENGUIN

Holly Webb

Illustrated by Polly Dunbar

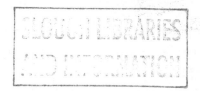

First published in Great Britain in 2011
by Scholastic Children's Books
This Large Print edition published 2012
by AudioGO Ltd
by arrangement with
Scholastic Limited

ISBN: 978 1445 89426 3

British Library Cataloguing in Publication Data available

Printed and bound in Great Britain by
MPG Books Group Limited

For Tom,

who has a fat cat of his own

1

Purring rumbled through the sleepy sunshine, and Alfie yawned again. It was a warm September Sunday afternoon, and he was full of lunch, and apples, and a squashed bar of chocolate that he'd forgotten was in the back pocket of his jeans. He settled himself more comfortably against the trunk of the apple tree and leaned his arm against the thick branch that jutted out in just the right place. Penguin, who was draped across the same branch like a fat furry rug, leaned forward a little and licked Alfie's elbow lovingly.

'Don't fall off,' Alfie murmured woozily. But it was a silly thing to say. Penguin never fell. He didn't look as though he was in the best shape for climbing trees—one would think his stomach would get in the

1

way, particularly for jumping. But Penguin had perfect balance, good even for a cat. Alfie smiled to himself as he remembered trying to persuade Penguin to walk along the washing line during the summer holidays. Penguin had refused, even for smoky bacon crisps, his favourite. (Although he had stolen the crisps off the table later.) Alfie had been convinced that Penguin would be a fabulous tightrope artist. They should try again. Perhaps it was the lack of circus music and Big Top atmosphere that had put him off. Maybe a costume . . . Alfie looked at Penguin thoughtfully. He wondered how easy it would be to get hold of a cat-shaped leotard.

Penguin opened one yellowish-golden eye a slit and stared sternly at Alfie, as though warning him that attempts to dress him in a sequinned cloak would result in severe scratches. But he didn't stop purring.

'OK,' Alfie murmured. 'But I bet it would be good for your tummy.'

Penguin ignored that. He didn't have any problems with the size of his stomach.

Penguin hadn't always been enormous. When Alfie had first found him, sitting on the front doorstep on the way home from school two years before, he had been very skinny indeed, and not much more than a kitten. Alfie was pretty sure he'd been a stray for a while, and that was why he loved food so much—he'd never been quite sure where the next meal was coming from.

Mum and Dad hadn't been at all sure about keeping the thin little black and white kitten, but Alfie had begged and begged. He had agreed to putting up posters, just in case someone else was looking for their lost cat, and he'd stood anxiously next to Mum as she had phoned all the vets in the local phonebook. But no one had turned up to claim the skinny kitten (who was already less skinny, after a couple of days of Alfie-sized meals). After two weeks, Mum and Dad had given in, and Alfie had announced the secret he'd been saving up.

The cat was called Penguin.

Dad had tried to explain that it was

ridiculous to call a cat that. He wasn't a penguin.

Alfie said he knew that quite well, thank you. The cat just looked like one. And it was true. Penguin had sleek black fur—getting sleeker by the day—and a shining white shirt front. When Alfie had spent his birthday money from Gran on a glow-in-the-dark orange collar, Penguin was a dead ringer for his namesake. When Alfie phoned Gran to tell her what he'd spent the money on, he had got a little parcel back with a silvery tag engraved with his phone number on one side and Penguin on the other. Gran liked cats. And even Dad could not argue now there was a collar with his name on.

Alfie sometimes wondered what would have happened if Penguin had chosen someone else's step to sit on that day. Where would he be now? It was impossible to imagine not having him there. Penguin was his best friend. Alfie had lots of friends at school, but he never talked to them as much as he talked to Penguin. Penguin was an excellent listener, and he always purred

4

in all the right places. Once, when Alfie was telling him about being kept in at lunch time by Mrs Haynes, the Year Two teacher he had never got on with, Penguin had coughed up a hairball all over the kitchen floor. Which just proved that he understood exactly what Alfie had been talking about.

Alfie liked Penguin plump. He thought it made him look even more penguin-like. But at his last check-up, the vet had suggested politely that Penguin ought to go on a diet, and Mum had bought a bag of special diet cat food. It did not look pleasant. Alfie hated the smell of the tins Penguin usually had, and forked it quickly into his bowl with his nose stuffed in the crook of his elbow. But at least the tinned stuff was meaty. Like something a proper cat might want to eat, after a hard day's prowling around after mice and birds. The diet version looked like rabbit poo.

Alfie had tried to explain to Mum that it wasn't going to work, but she hadn't been in a very good mood, as his baby sister Jess had just thrown a bowlful of lovingly mashed carrots into the toaster.

'If he doesn't like it, he won't eat it,' she'd snapped, trying to fish the orange goo out with a spoon. 'And that'll have the same effect in the long run. Stop fussing, Alfie!'

Alfie had sighed, and measured the correct, tiny amount of diet food into Penguin's bowl. It didn't even cover the fish pattern on the bottom. Alfie had crossed his fingers behind his back and set it down in front of Penguin, who was coiling himself adoringly around Alfie's ankles.

Penguin had stopped dead, and stared up at Alfie accusingly.

'Sorry! The vet said!' Alfie protested. 'Your legs are going to start hurting if you don't go on a diet.'

Penguin sniffed suspiciously at the little brown pellets, then turned round and went straight out of the cat flap.

Later that evening, two sausages mysteriously disappeared while Alfie's mum wasn't looking.

The diet cat food lasted about a week before Mum binned it. She told

Alfie that it was expensive anyway, but since she'd now had to replace most of what was in the fridge as well, it was like feeding three cats instead of one.

Penguin sat on one of the kitchen chairs looking happily plump and watched as she put the rest of the bag into the bin.

'That cat is smirking at me!' Mum said crossly, as she clanged the bin shut. 'This really can't go on, Alfie. It's for his own good!'

'I don't think he thinks he's fat,' Alfie explained.

'You'll just have to make sure he gets more exercise.' Mum sniffed. 'Maybe you should put a sausage on a string and make him chase it up and down the garden.'

Now, looking at Penguin's stomach gently folding over the edges of the branch, Alfie had to admit he was larger than he should be. But it was hard to make a cat exercise when he didn't want to. Alfie had tried racing up and down the garden, and even throwing a bouncy ball for Penguin to chase. Penguin had sat on the garden bench, eyeing him with fascinated interest, as though he wondered why Alfie was bothering. After all, it wasn't as if he was a dog.

'It'll be tea time soon,' Alfie murmured. From his position in the tree, he could just about see into their kitchen window next door, and it looked like Mum was pottering about making sandwiches with leftover chicken. He yawned. 'We'll go back home in a minute.' He had to be careful to get back before Mum or Dad came looking for him—nobody knew that he was in next door's garden.

Alfie and Penguin had found the loose board in the fence a little while after Penguin had arrived on Alfie's doorstep. Alfie had been so excited about having a cat that for a few weeks he had followed Penguin everywhere, and Penguin hadn't seemed to mind. Alfie had rolled underneath every bed in the house (although he didn't fit under the sofa like Penguin did), wedged himself into the airing cupboard, and gone crawling through the flower beds down at the bottom of

8

the garden.

Penguin particularly liked the flower beds. It had been late summer when he arrived and the weather had been horribly hot. Penguin had spent a lot of time collapsed under bushes, and Alfie had collapsed under them with him. They had watched, fascinated, as ants crawled past their noses and dry leaves tickled their ears.

When they weren't slumped in the heat, they'd investigated every scrap of the garden, and it was behind the shed that they had made the discovery— the loose board, swinging from a nail where it had been badly mended once before. It was like a perfect little cat-and-boy-sized doorway. It had taken a couple of days for Alfie to pluck up the courage to go through it. He didn't know much about the old lady next door, only her name, Mrs Barratt, and a few other odd little snippets. Mum had said she was ill, and couldn't walk very far, not even up the stairs in her house. Dad moaned about the brambles snaking under the fence from her garden, and Mum told him off for being unkind, when the poor lady couldn't really get out there with her garden tools, could she?

So Alfie knew that Mrs Barratt hardly ever went into her garden. And that it was overgrown enough to hide in. It was the perfect place for exploring.

At first Alfie and Penguin had followed tunnels through the brambles, Alfie tearing his shorts and staining his fingers and lips scarlet with squishy-ripe blackberries. They'd prowled through next door's garden like a pair of panthers, Alfie loving the feel of being somewhere he shouldn't really be, and Penguin pouncing on shadows like the overgrown kitten he was.

Alfie's own garden didn't have anything to explore. It was neat and divided up into what Mum called garden rooms. Lots of little hedges, and screens, and statues that popped up and surprised you. But it was so neat, it was useless for having adventures in.

The only good thing about it was that Mum could never quite tell which part of the garden Alfie was in. If he heard her calling him, it was easy to suggest he'd just been lurking behind the sweet peas, when actually he'd slipped back through the loose board, and emerged from behind the shed looking innocent.

Then one afternoon, a few weeks after they'd first ventured into the wilderness, Alfie and Penguin had discovered the tree. It was a huge old apple tree down at the far end of the garden, where it backed on to a little wood. The apple tree's furthest branches joined the elderberries on the other side of the fence. It was first time they'd explored that far and the ground around the tree had been buzzing with drunken wasps, feeding on the fallen apples. Penguin had sniffed one, and jumped back in shock when it buzzed angrily at him, and flew wobbling away.

Alfie had stood staring up at the trunk, wondering if he could climb it. He could reach the first branch with his hands, but he'd never get a foot up there. He'd always wanted a treehouse. He supposed Mrs Barratt might notice

if he built a house in her tree, but then Mum had said her eyesight wasn't very good. Surely she wouldn't notice him hidden in the branches? The next time he came through the fence, Alfie brought an old wooden box that had been round the back of the shed by the compost heap for ages. With that he could just scramble far enough up to get his elbows over the first branch.

He needed to grow. His mum was always complaining that he grew out of things—now for the first time Alfie was actually trying to grow on purpose. He started drinking more milk, but gave up after a week as it didn't seem to work. He went back to the tree every

day and stood underneath it, eyeing the huge branches. He would be able to see everything from up there. As far as his friend Oliver's house down the road, he thought. Maybe even further. But he still couldn't reach that vital first branch.

It was soon after then that Alfie found the rope. It was quite close to the house, which was probably why he hadn't seen it before. He didn't normally like to go too close, in case Mrs Barratt spotted him. He occasionally saw her, just a smudge behind the kitchen window blind, but no more. He wasn't quite sure if that made her more scary or less. Alfie sometimes pretended she was a witch hidden behind the windows and if she caught him in her garden she would put him under an evil spell. It made the challenge of climbing the tree—a witch's tree—even more exciting.

Alfie had heard her scolding Penguin through her window as well, telling him off for sitting on the fence and staring hungrily at the birds on her feeders.

It was one afternoon when he'd been trying to distract Penguin from the birds that Alfie spotted the rope. And it was the rope that got Alfie into the tree.

2

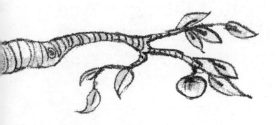

'Alfie! Alfie!' Mum was calling from the kitchen door. Alfie stopped daydreaming and peered down between the branches to check that she wasn't looking over into Mrs Barratt's garden. Then he slid quickly down the tree trunk, hardly using the rope at all. He was a lot taller than he had been two years ago, and the tree was easy to climb into now.

Penguin followed him, loping from branch to branch and springing down into the long grass. In the two years since they'd discovered the wilderness next door, it had only grown thicker and wilder. Every so often, Alfie borrowed Mum's kitchen scissors to cut himself a way through the brambles, but they grew back like something out of a fairy tale. He was used to getting scratched; it was worth it, to have a whole land of adventure and mystery all to himself.

They shot back through the fence and emerged, wandering carelessly up their own garden.

'Hey, Mum.'

'Oh, there you are! Tea's ready, Alfie. Just some sandwiches. And please don't feed them to the cat— you know it's not good for him.' She frowned down the garden. 'Where were you?'

Alfie shrugged. 'Just playing down at the bottom. There's a massive spider hanging on a web outside the shed, did you know?'

Mum shuddered. She hated spiders, and the shed terrified her—she had to go in there to get her spades and things, but she did it at a run, not really looking, in case she saw one of the family of huge spiders that lived in the corners. They liked to lurk around the tools and pop out at her. If Alfie was around, she sent him to get the tools for her. Alfie quite liked spiders, but he tried not to get too close, because Penguin always wanted to hunt them. Alfie had seen him several times sitting by the shed looking rather embarrassed, with legs trailing out of the corners of his mouth like a set of extra whiskers. Alfie thought spiders must be tickly to swallow—they seemed to take a lot of gulping.

Still, the spider distracted Mum from wondering where he'd been.

'Couldn't you feed it to Penguin?' she asked.

'Mum! I don't think they're good for him. Besides, you wanted him on a diet—no snacks, you said!'

'I shouldn't think spiders are very fattening, Alfie. And he'd probably have to run around to catch it.'

Penguin twirled himself around her legs, purring, and Mum laughed. 'Yes, you'd like to eat me up a horrible spider, wouldn't you? Come on, Alfie, I left Jess with a sandwich, she's probably wrecked the kitchen by now.'

But Jess was still sitting angelically in her high chair, clapping her hands as Dad sang her 'London's Burning'. It was her favourite song, but only he was allowed to sing it for her. It was as if she knew he was a firefighter.

'I saw Mrs Barratt from next door earlier on,' Mum mentioned as she passed Alfie a sandwich.

Alfie nearly dropped it. Had Mrs Barratt seen him? Had she complained that he'd been messing around in her garden?

'I haven't seen her for weeks . . .' Dad murmured through a mouthful of chicken sandwich, not noticing Alfie's rabbit-in-the-headlights gaze. 'Is she all right?'

'Yes, she's fine. She waved to me as I was walking past with Jess in the pushchair. She was just saying goodbye to the meals on wheels people. But she won't be needing them soon, she said. She was very excited about it.'

'She's not going into sheltered housing, is she?' Dad asked. 'She always said she couldn't bear the thought of it. She loves that house, even if she hasn't seen most of it for years.'

Mum smiled. 'No, nothing like that. Her daughter's coming to live with her!'

Dad frowned. 'Really? The one she never sees? That's a surprise.'

Dad did look quite surprised, but it was nothing compared to how Alfie felt. A daughter! That would be someone around Mum's age, probably. Someone who'd be bound to go upstairs, and look out of the windows, and maybe even try and sort out the jungle of a garden.

'I think Mrs Barratt didn't get on

with Lucy's husband,' Mum explained. 'But now they've split up, and Lucy's coming to stay with her mother for a while. And the best bit is, Lucy's got a daughter your age, Alfie. She's missed the first week of school, of course, but you'll have someone next door to play with, isn't that great?'

Alfie blinked, and Penguin took the opportunity to snatch a bit of chicken that was dangling from his sandwich.

A girl? Next door? Why was this supposed to be good news?

*　　*　　*

'She's coming this week sometime. She'll probably go to our school!' Alfie hissed, panicked, to Oliver the next morning, as they spilled out of the classroom at break.

Oliver nodded. 'Mm, probably. But it's not that bad—Alice and Emily in Year Two live next door to me. I don't have to hang around with them or anything. Their mum brings me home sometimes, that's all.'

Alfie snorted. He didn't want some

strange girl and her mum bringing him home. And he didn't want anyone in his garden.

That was the real problem. It wasn't his garden. It never had been. And now he was going to have to give it up.

Oliver frowned suddenly, his dark eyebrows meeting in the middle like furry caterpillars. 'What about your tree?' Oliver came over to Alfie's house every couple of weeks or so, and Alfie had shown him the loose board and the garden next door—after making him swear an elaborate oath of secrecy that had a lot to do with a book about pirates that he'd just read. Oliver was suitably envious of the tree— he only had a baby playhouse in his garden. With curtains.

Alfie stared at him. He felt as though Oliver wasn't understanding on purpose. 'It won't be my tree, will it?' he snapped. 'It'll be her tree now!' He stomped off, barging Oliver out of the way with his shoulder, and not caring if it hurt. It was Oliver's fault for being so stupid.

Luckily, Oliver was thick-skinned, and just elbowed Alfie in the ribs at lunch time as a way of getting him back. 'No girl's going to get through all those brambles to the tree,' he pointed out. 'You'll just have to be careful to stay out of her way, that's all.'

Alfie nodded gratefully.

But Oliver had underestimated the girl next door.

Alfie slid out into the garden when he got home, before Mum could mention homework, or watching Jess while she made dinner. Penguin was asleep in the ironing basket and didn't seem to want to move, so for once Alfie set off down the garden alone. Even after Oliver had told him not to worry, he still felt miserable as he pushed the board back. Like it might be the last time. He wriggled through the gap, wormed his way along below the level of the brambles and hauled himself up into the tree. The bark was rough against his fingers, but he didn't care. He settled himself on to his favourite branch and eyed the apple he'd been watching for the past few days. It was a sharp yellowish-green all over, with just a faint brownish flush. Almost perfectly ripe, he thought. And even if it wasn't, he didn't want to leave it, in case the girl could climb trees. He twisted it off the stalk, and it came away easily—it was ripe, then.

Alfie leaned back against the tree trunk and stared at the house. Mum hadn't said exactly when Lucy and the girl were coming—but then Jess was teething, and she'd been having a screaming day. He'd ask Mum later if she'd heard anything. He bit into the apple thoughtfully. He would be like a spy in enemy territory. Penguin could be his scout cat. He grinned to himself at the idea of Penguin wearing a bulletproof vest.

'Did you know you're stealing that apple?'

Alfie nearly fell out of the tree. The voice had come from up above him. He stared up, blinking against the sunlight filtering down through the branches.

Someone was sitting higher up the

tree, astride the slightly wobbly branch that Alfie tended to avoid.

'In fact, you're trespassing. This is my gran's garden.'

Alfie opened his mouth to defend himself, and then shut it again. She was quite right. What on earth could he say?

'I bet she doesn't mind,' he muttered weakly.

'Did you ask her?' The girl lay down along the branch to look at him better, and it bounced in a way that made Alfie's stomach bounce too.

'You need to be careful with that branch,' he muttered. If she fell out of the tree while he was there, Alfie had a strong feeling that she was one of those girls who'd make sure he got into trouble for it.

'No, I don't,' she snapped back. 'I'm fine. Bet you couldn't get up here.'

The girl wriggled her way along the branch, her blonde hair hanging downwards. She was wearing jeans and a pale pink T-shirt, now streaked with lichen all down the front.

'That branch isn't strong enough at

25

the end.' Alfie stood up, very carefully, wriggling his feet to the best place on the branch and hanging on to the one above him. She needed to get down. He held a hand out to her. 'Come back down. You have to.'

'Get lost.' The girl smirked. She bounced up and down on purpose, and the whole tree shuddered. Alfie's foot slipped, and his stomach slid sideways. He gasped. He was going to be sick. He loved the tree, and he was good at climbing, but he liked to be holding on tight.

He grabbed the trunk to steady himself and felt the apple slip out of his hand. Alfie didn't want to be in the tree any longer. He grabbed the rope and flung himself down, grazing the side of his leg against the bark.

'Good! You run away! And stay out of my garden!' the girl yelled after him.

Her garden now, he noticed. Not even her gran's.

But really, the only thing that mattered was that it wasn't Alfie's any more.

3

'This is Grace, everyone. She's just moved here, and she'll be joining our class.'

She stood up at the front of the classroom next to Mrs Cartwright, the long blonde hair now pulled back in two neat bunches. They made her look like a dog with long ears.

Alfie huddled down in his seat, hoping to avoid her eye. His leg still hurt, and he'd had to tell Mum he slipped on the path. But Mrs Cartwright was looking straight at him and smiling. 'Alfie, I think Grace is living very close to you, isn't she?'

Alfie nodded reluctantly. He couldn't really do anything else.

'Lovely. Well, we'll put Grace on your table, and you and Oliver and Asha and Sammie can look after her for the minute.' Mrs Cartwright ushered Grace towards Alfie's table— why did they have to have an empty chair? Then she turned back to the whiteboard and started talking about their Romans topic again.

Grace stared at Alfie. Her eyes were bluish-green, he noticed, now that he wasn't staring up into the sunlight.

'Hello, Alfie . . .' she said, her voice rather nastily sweet.

'Is that her?' Oliver muttered. 'From next door?' Alfie hadn't told him about the meeting in the tree—he was too embarrassed.

Alfie nodded. 'You want that book for making your story plan in,' he muttered to Grace. 'The blue one.' He'd only get into trouble with Mrs Cartwright if he didn't look after her properly, however much he felt like directing her into the boys' toilets.

She was staring at him as he turned back to the board again. Her eyes looked like the pieces of sea glass he'd picked up on the beach on their summer holiday. Hard and greenish and shiny. Worn away by years of water, but still bright. He had the pieces lined up on his window sill. He'd move them when he got home, he decided.

Luckily, she went off with Asha and Sammie at lunch time, and he didn't have to do anything about her. At the end of the day, he came out of school heaving a sigh that seemed to leave all of him feeling lighter. He'd stay in the house this afternoon, he decided. Even if it was still tropical-hot.

His mum waved at him from the playground. She was standing next to a woman with short, spiky blonde hair and familiar bluish-green eyes. The woman was cuddling Jess.

Alfie slowed right down. Mum had gone and made friends with Grace's mother.

How could she? It was treachery. But he supposed she didn't know.

His mum was smiling as he trailed towards them. 'Look, Alfie—this is Lucy, from next door.'

Alfie tried to smile, but it came out more like a wolf baring its teeth. Grace's mother looked slightly

29

surprised, but she still smiled back. 'Hi, Alfie. It's nice to meet you. Was Grace OK today?'

He nodded. 'Um, yeah. She's made friends with Asha in our class. Asha's nice.'

'I've asked Lucy to bring Grace back to ours for tea,' Mum said, smiling brightly, in that way she had that suggested Alfie needed to sort his manners out.

Grace came walking across the playground towards them. Alfie thought she hesitated as she spotted him, but then she pasted on a smile. 'Hi, Mrs Seton.'

Alfie blinked. She'd met his mum already then. It seemed as though she hadn't said anything to her about the tree—or was she about to now?

Grace gave her mum a hug, and her mum explained about tea at Alfie's. Grace nodded, and stuck her tongue out at Alfie when no one else was looking.

Alfie made a low growling noise, and then tried to look as though it was his stomach rumbling when his mum turned round and glared at him. He shrugged and looked innocently at her, but he could see she wasn't convinced.

Back home, Alfie put the TV on. He wasn't really supposed to watch it straight after school, but he reckoned with guests around Mum wouldn't make a fuss. He and Grace sat at opposite ends of the sofa, not talking, and pretending to watch the programme. He could hear Mum chatting to Lucy in the kitchen, just the odd word here and there. They sounded like old friends.

Grace was listening too. She scowled as she heard her mother laugh loudly at something Alfie's mum had said. 'I should make you pay for that apple you stole.'

Alfie gaped at her. 'What?'

'A pound.'

'Apples don't cost that much!' Alfie protested, realizing, too late, that he should have said he wouldn't pay anything at all.

'Stolen ones do.'

'Oh, shut up,' Alfie snapped. It wasn't a very clever answer, but he couldn't think of anything better right now. Besides, she was just so annoying!

'Don't tell me to shut up! I bet your mum doesn't know you were in my garden.' Grace swung her bunches, smiling a superior smile.

'Yes, she does,' Alfie growled. But he'd gone scarlet, he knew it. He was a terrible liar. The tree was the only thing he'd ever been able to get away with, because Mum and Dad had never asked him about it.

He wished Penguin was there for him to stroke. He was probably asleep on Alfie's bed.

'Alfie! Grace! Come and have some tea!'

Alfie stood up, racing for the door and nearly crashing into Grace on the way. They wrestled in the doorway for a minute, hissing insults, and Grace shot out towards the kitchen. Alfie followed her, glowering.

He could hear a series of light thumps on the stairs—Penguin coming down them with his funny lolloping jump. He'd heard Alfie's mum calling too, and he knew what tea meant.

Alfie's frown faded, and he crouched down to stroke Penguin under the chin. The big cat purred hungrily, peering past him to the kitchen.

Feeling better now he had his sidekick, Alfie strolled into the kitchen. Mum had done pizza for tea, which was one of his favourites. He slid into a seat as far from Grace as possible, and Penguin took up his station by Alfie's feet.

'Could you pour Grace some juice, Alfie?' Mum asked. She was giving him a look again. Alfie nodded, resisting the temptation to pour it all over Grace's school dress.

Penguin's face appeared at the side of his chair, looking hopeful. He specialized in a pitiful round-eyed stare that made him look as if he was starving to death, and he knew Alfie found it hard to resist.

Alfie sneaked a scrap of ham off his pizza and held it under the table, trying not to laugh as Penguin's rough tongue scraped his fingers eagerly.

The problem with feeding Penguin at the table was that when Alfie did it once, it only made the cat beg for more. Insistent paws kept patting Alfie's leg, and every so often Penguin would press his chilly little nose into the hollow of Alfie's knee, making him wriggle as he tried not to laugh.

Mum and Lucy were too busy chatting to notice, and Jess was carefully shredding a piece of pizza

into crumbs, but Grace was watching him, Alfie realized. He stared back at her coldly, and she dropped a bit of garlic bread on purpose, so she could peer under the table.

She came face to face with Penguin, and gasped. 'You've got a cat!'

'Genius!' Alfie muttered under his breath. Then he added, 'He's called

Penguin,' to earn himself some brownie points with Mum.

Mum smiled at her. 'Yes, he was a stray. He arrived on our doorstep a couple of years ago. He's lovely, but he's a bit overweight, so try not to drop anything—he'll be there in seconds!'

Grace nodded solemnly, pretending not to know that Penguin was hoovering up her dropped garlic bread that very minute.

Penguin prowled happily under the table for the rest of the meal, as Grace and Alfie competed to feed him the best bits of pizza. He followed them when they left the table, his whiskers glistening with cheese grease and his ears at a smug, jaunty angle.

Alfie and Grace went back to their places on the sofa, and he hopped up between them. Both of them wriggled closer to stroke him, and Penguin settled down purring, his eyes half closed.

Alfie watched Grace tickling Penguin behind the ears, and grudgingly admitted to himself that she knew cats. It was Penguin's favourite place to be rubbed, and his purr was deepening into the low, sleepy noise he made when he was really happy.

He liked her!

It wasn't fair.

Penguin definitely wouldn't let just anyone mess with his ears like that. He'd clawed Alfie's cousin Rosie's hand when she'd tried it. Mum had been really cross, and made Alfie put Penguin out in the garden and lock the cat flap, even though it was pouring with rain. Alfie had sneaked out after a while and found Penguin sulking under a bush. They'd hidden out in the shed together, hunting spiders till Rosie and Auntie Jen had gone.

If Penguin was going to sleep with Grace stroking his ears, maybe she wasn't that bad after all. Or maybe he was just so stuffed full of pizza that he'd sleep even if she was knitting with his tail.

4

'Penguin!' Alfie thumped up the stairs to check his room the next evening—Mum had a habit of shutting the door for tidiness' sake and accidentally shutting Penguin in. But Penguin wasn't mewing furiously behind his door, and he wasn't even asleep on Alfie's bed. Alfie thundered back down again, and out into the garden. It was very unusual for Penguin to be late for tea.

He wandered round the garden, checking Penguin's favourite sun-bathing places—the stone bench, and the wall next to the bird table, which combined sun and snacks (or so Penguin seemed to hope). Alfie had never actually seen him catch a bird from the bird table. But he liked to lie there watching while the birds twittered and muttered and complained about him.

No Penguin. Alfie stood in the middle of the tiny square of lawn, looking worriedly up and down the garden. Where on earth was he? Alfie usually fed him at about five, and it was past that now.

The garden seemed full of early evening shadows and strange bright patches, and suddenly Alfie whirled round, sure that someone was watching him. And laughing!

'Here, Harry. Have another one.' It was the slightest whisper, from over by the fence. No—the other side of the fence. There was purring too, Penguin's strange low purr.

'Good boy. Is that nice?' Someone laughed, quietly, and Alfie seethed. It was Grace, of course. She had Penguin in her garden. And what was she doing calling him Harry?

Alfie grabbed a bucket that someone had left by the bench and crept over to the fence, turning the bucket upside down and standing on it, so that he could just see over.

It looked like Grace's mum had already started trying to tidy up the garden. There was definitely more path than there had been. From his spy point over the fence, Alfie could see a flash of blue-checked dress through the brambles. Grace's school uniform. And a white-tipped black tail was twitching excitedly next to her.

Alfie jumped down and raced to the end of the garden and the loose board—for once without even checking whether Mum was watching him.

He flung himself behind the shed and tried to dive through the loose board, desperate to get Penguin back.

Grace jumped up as she heard the creak of the board swinging back. 'You're not allowed in my garden!' she shouted.

'You're not allowed to play with my cat!' Alfie yelled back. He'd somehow managed to get himself wedged in the hole; his elbow was caught, and he felt stupid and furious. 'Penguin, tea time, come on!'

Penguin edged curiously around the clump of brambles, eyeing Alfie as

40

though he'd never seen such a strange beast before.

'Are you stuck in the fence?' Grace giggled. 'You must have had too much school lunch. I didn't think anyone actually ate that disgusting turkey hotpot.'

Alfie wriggled desperately. He was so embarrassed. He was supposed to be telling her off, not making her laugh! His elbow was really hurting, and he couldn't even work out how he'd managed to get stuck.

'You look so funny!' Grace was standing there with her hand over her mouth, laughing at him. Alfie was sure that if he hadn't been stuck he would have kicked her. He gave one more huge heave, backwards this time, and fell back through the fence, ripping his shirt sleeve and clutching his scraped arm.

There was a scrabble and a thump, and Penguin appeared on top of the fence, peering down curiously. He mewed and jumped down, nosing lovingly at Alfie. Alfie picked him up, a warm, saggy bundle of fur—Penguin was slipping through Alfie's arms like a beanbag toy. But Alfie wasn't going to let him go.

Grace slid the board back and watched him through the hole.

'Leave Penguin alone!' Alfie growled, hitching him up.

Penguin mewed reproachfully but didn't wriggle.

'That's a really stupid name for a cat,' Grace told him, her voice calm and sweet. Her school uniform looked pristine. Alfie wondered if he could manage to sneak back inside and hide his shirt somewhere. Mum was going to make a huge fuss about the state of his clothes.

'It isn't, and it's none of your business what he's called. You shouldn't be calling him anything,' he snapped at her, backing out of the gap behind the shed.

He raced up the garden, Penguin dangling in his arms, and slammed the kitchen door behind him. Then he locked the cat flap. Penguin was his cat. That girl wasn't going anywhere near him. Wasn't it enough that she'd already had his tree?

*　　　*　　　*

'Alfie, bedtime!'

Alfie backed out of the understairs

cupboard, scowling. 'I can't go to bed, Mum, I haven't found Penguin. I haven't seen him since after tea.'

Alfie had a horrible suspicion he knew where Penguin was. It had been two days since he'd caught Grace feeding him cat treats, and since then he'd been watching Penguin every moment he could. But cats aren't easy to guard, and Penguin had slipped out when Mum insisted on Alfie having a bath.

'He's probably out in the garden. Go and call him.'

Alfie sighed. Mum wasn't paying attention—she was trying to get Jess to go down, and Jess wasn't, which meant Mum had at most half an ear on anything Alfie was trying to say.

'Mum! I have called him! I've called and called. I've looked everywhere. What do you think I was doing in the cupboard?'

Mum shrugged, smiling. 'Last time you went in that cupboard you told me you were a prehistoric caveman and it was your cave. Penguin was a sabre-toothed tiger. How was I supposed to know, Alfie?'

Alfie huffed. That had been weeks ago. 'I've called him, and I've shaken the box of cat treats for ages in the garden. He always comes when I do that. I'm really worried about him, Mum.'

There was another wail from upstairs, and Mum flinched. 'Alfie, cats like to wander. Especially at night. Penguin will be back soon, I'm sure. Go and brush your teeth, sweetheart.'

She already had her foot on the first step of the stairs, and Alfie knew she was too worried about Jess to listen properly. He slipped back into the kitchen, peering out of the window into the darkening garden and hoping to hear the clatter of the cat flap as Penguin squeezed himself back inside.

Alfie was pretty sure that Grace had Penguin with her next door now. She worked fast.

He trailed up the stairs, past the still-wailing Jess, and crawled under his duvet.

He wondered if Penguin was asleep on Grace's bed.

45

The next morning, Alfie woke up, and realized happily that it was Saturday. Although there was something not good happening. He couldn't yet remember what. It was the feeling he usually got about spelling tests, but since it was the weekend, that obviously wasn't it.

He reached out to stroke Penguin, stretched down the side of the bed like he always was—Dad always said that Penguin was trying to beat the record for the world's longest cat.

Penguin wasn't there.

Alfie swallowed, his mouth suddenly feeling sour. Of course. For just a minute he'd forgotten that Penguin had never come home.

What if it wasn't Grace? What if Penguin had been run over? It had happened to a cat who lived down the road. Penguin didn't usually go out at the front of the house—but then he didn't usually stay away overnight, either. Alfie shook his head briskly. It was easier to be angry and believe it was Grace.

It was eight o'clock. Too early to go next door and demand his cat back. Alfie decided to do it anyway.

Mum and Dad were still asleep, or at any rate he couldn't hear any noise from their room. Alfie padded swiftly downstairs, unlocked the front door and marched the few steps along the pavement to Mrs Barratt's house. There were net curtains across the living-room window, but Alfie was pretty sure he saw someone dart across the room as he came up to the front door. It opened before he could ring the bell, and Grace was standing there in pink shorts and a T-shirt—or that's what it looked like. She'd opened the door the tiniest crack, only wide enough for him to see one eye.

'Go away!'

'Where's Penguin?' Alfie pushed the door angrily. If she wasn't hiding anything, why wouldn't she open the door properly?

'You're going to disturb my gran!' Grace tried to push the door closed

47

again, but Alfie barged it with his shoulder.

'You've got him—you stole him!' he said. 'Give him back!'

'Ssshh! Shut up!' The door opened properly at last, and a skinny hand grabbed his sleeve and hauled him inside. Alfie was so shocked he half fell over, and Penguin jumped on him, purring happily.

Grace yanked him upright and hurried him into the little front room he'd seen her in through the nets. Penguin trotted after them, waving his tail.

'You're not to shout, don't you get it? My gran's not very well; we're not supposed to wake her up. And my mum's still asleep too.'

'Oh.' Alfie nodded. 'Sorry.' Then he shook his head, feeling as though good manners had just spoiled his attack. 'Don't tell me not to shout anyway!' he retorted, but in a sort of hoarse whisper. 'I'm allowed to shout, you stole my cat.'

'I did not.' Grace sat down on an armchair by the window, and stroked

Penguin, who was washing carelessly, close to her feet. 'He came in the garden. I suppose he's used to being in there, because you trespassed so much.'

Alfie flushed, his cheeks suddenly burning. She was so right he couldn't even argue.

'You made him come in the house,' he muttered. He wasn't entirely sure about this, but he didn't think Penguin would have gone in on his own.

She shook her head virtuously, and he was almost certain she was lying. Her eyes changed, and she didn't look at him, quite. 'He followed me.' Then she looked up, shrugging. 'You have to let him do what he wants. You can't train a cat.' She looked down at Penguin, who bumped his head against her sandal affectionately. 'I can't help it that he likes me, can I? He wanted to explore, that's all. It's like the call of the wild.'

'No, it isn't!' Alfie leaned over quickly and grabbed the shiny foil packet that he'd just spotted half-hidden by the cushions behind. 'More like the call of the cat treats! You saw we had this kind at our house, and you went and bought some so you could bribe him into coming over here!'

Grace snatched them back, stuffing them down behind the cushions again, and Penguin stopped licking his paws and watched the progress of the foil packet with interest. He knew exactly what was in there.

'Those are mine,' Grace muttered.

'Oh, you eat them, do you? Tuna's your favourite, then?'

'If Penguin wants to come over here, you can't stop him,' Grace said fiercely. 'He isn't even yours. He was a stray. Your mum said so. He just turned up at your house. Well, now he's turned up at mine, hasn't he? Maybe he likes our house better.'

Alfie shook his head and looked down at Penguin, who'd given up on the hope of treats and was washing again. He couldn't, could he? He wouldn't abandon Alfie, who'd looked after him for two whole years? 'Penguin,' he whispered. 'Come on. Let's go home.'

Penguin glanced up at him but didn't move.

'Penguin,' Alfie tried again, his voice rising to a frightened half-squeak. 'Home. Let's go.'

'He doesn't have to go with you unless he wants to,' Grace started smugly, and Alfie stepped back towards the door, knowing he was about to cry and not wanting her to see. But Penguin got up and followed him, overtaking and trotting ahead out into the hallway. Alfie ran after him, his heart thudding and skipping in relief, and wrestled with the door catch.

He looked back as he flung it open and saw Grace standing in the door of the front room, clutching the cat treats and looking as miserable as he'd felt a minute before.

Alfie felt quite guilty—for about ten seconds. Then he decided it was all her own fault.

5

But Alfie's relief didn't last. He told himself it was only because of the cat treats, but Penguin kept popping round to Grace's house. He was starting to look even plumper than he had before, and he actually turned down breakfast once, which left even Mum looking shocked.

'Goodness, he must be getting food from somewhere else!' she commented, looking at the full bowl, and Penguin wedging himself into the cat flap. He really had to heave to get through now.

'Mum! I told you! Grace keeps feeding him treats. She's trying to steal him.'

'Don't be silly, Alfie.'

'It isn't silly! She really is, Mum. She kept him at her house overnight last weekend. She wants him to be hers.

She even said so! She said he wasn't really ours because he was a stray.'

'Alfie . . .'

Alfie knew that tone. It was his mum's sensible voice, and it meant she didn't believe a word he said.

'Why don't you ever believe me?' he yelled, all his worry about Penguin and his anger with Grace coming out in one furious shout. 'You don't love Penguin; you never have. You didn't even want me to have him. You wouldn't care if he went and lived at Grace's house, even if it did make me miserable. You don't even love me!'

'Alfie!' Dad walked in from the living room, where he'd been reading to Jess. He looked really annoyed. 'Don't talk to your mum like that!'

'Oh, Alfie . . .' His mother folded her arms and stared down at him, shaking her head as if she thought he was just having a silly tantrum.

Alfie stamped his feet, and his throat felt rough, as if the words were tearing out of him. He glared at Mum and Dad. 'You don't love me or Penguin, Mum! You said he was a something nuisance, and that's a word you told me I was never, ever, ever, ever allowed to say.'

Dad made a strange sort of snorting noise. He was laughing! Alfie felt like he was about to burst—it wasn't funny!

His mother rolled her eyes. 'Alfie, he had just torn a pigeon to pieces in my bathroom!' she hissed. 'I think I'm allowed to be annoyed!'

Alfie was never quite sure how Penguin had managed that. He must have dragged the pigeon into the house through the cat flap, hauled it up the stairs, and then played with it rather messily all over the bathroom. It was a large pigeon too. It had been a bit of a shock for Mum walking in on it.

'You're glad he's gone to Grace's!' Alfie snarled. 'I hate you!'

'Go to your room!' Mum finally snapped, and Alfie stomped heavily out of the kitchen, kicking the door on the way, because he knew it would really annoy her.

'Just because he gets hairs on your black trousers!' he yelled as he hurled himself up the stairs. 'You care more about trousers than you do about me!'

*　　　*　　　*

Penguin didn't come back to Alfie's that night either—which Alfie couldn't help feeling was ungrateful, when Alfie had bothered to get sent to bed defending his honour.

But then he was back at Alfie's house for the rest of the week, and things were just as they had always been. Penguin even played football with him on Saturday morning. Alfie had an important match on Sunday, and he was practising in the garden. Penguin was sitting on the bench looking miffed—no birds were going to be on the feeder with Alfie kicking a ball around. His whiskers trembled with irritation, until Alfie came and sat down beside him, panting. 'Sorry, Penguin. I've got to practise. We can't let Purlham beat us again, and I'm in goal since Max broke his leg.'

Penguin butted his arm lovingly, yawned, and jumped off the bench, looking expectantly back at Alfie.

He nosed the ball, then jumped on it, rolling over and over like a kitten going mad with a ball of paper. Alfie laughed. Penguin hadn't done that in ages. 'Handball, Penguin! Or pawball . . . Although I suppose actually you've got four feet. Maybe you're allowed.' He chased after Penguin and the ball, and they dodged and weaved all over the garden. Penguin was particularly good at a sort of four-paw sliding tackle.

They had such a good time that Alfie was starting to hope that Penguin had just been nosing at Grace's house. Maybe now the excitement had worn off.

Then Penguin disappeared that night, and didn't come back.

It ruined Alfie's weekend. Sunday afternoon's football match was a disaster. Alfie's team were playing Purlham All Stars, who'd beaten them last year, and everyone was desperate for revenge.

But Alfie let in three goals, and Sam Kelly's mum said very loudly, right in front of half the rest of the team—who all told Alfie about it—that Alfie was a disgrace and shouldn't be allowed to play.

The only good bit of the day was Mum telling Mrs Kelly that when Sam stopped scoring own goals maybe she'd have a right to be rude about

everybody else. Dad had to hurry her away before Mrs Kelly managed to work through her shock and think of anything else to say.

Alfie arrived at school on Monday hoping for something fun to happen to take his mind off the football disaster. He still had a horrible feeling people might be pointing and sniggering, but Oliver told him to stop being dim. 'We'll beat them next year. And anyway, my dad said their striker looked as though he was about thirteen; there's no way he should have been in the under-tens league.'

Alfie nodded gratefully. He supposed it didn't really matter that much. Hopefully he'd never have to be in goal again . . .

They went into class to be greeted by Mrs Cartwright announcing a Project. They'd only had Mrs Cartwright for about three weeks, but she was known for her Projects. Year Three were learning about the Romans, and Mrs Cartwright was so excited she was practically frothing at the mouth. Gladiators! Feasts! Dormice!

Big forks! Alfie blinked wearily as it all rolled over his head. He liked the sound of Romans—although he didn't quite get where the dormice fitted in—but he hadn't slept very well the previous night. He kept reliving the disastrous football match, and then worrying about Penguin.

He zoned in again when he heard his name mentioned. It was a survival tactic that he'd learned in Year Two. He looked up, wide-eyed, trying to seem innocent. What? Was he being told off?

'. . . and Grace . . . Lily and Maddie-Mae. Robin and Elsie . . .'

Oh. Only a list of people to work with then. Alfie stopped worrying, and then realized what Mrs Cartwright had said. He had to work with Grace.

He glanced over at her. She looked blank, and ducked her eyes when she saw him looking at her. Probably she felt guilty about Penguin being at her house right now, Alfie thought, folding his arms and glaring.

Mrs Cartwright put a film about Romans on the whiteboard after that, so there was no working with Grace to be done before lunch time. But when they came back in from the playground, she told them to sit with their new partners.

Alfie scowled stubbornly at Grace. He wasn't moving from his place. She'd just have to come and sit next to him. He saw her wrinkle her nose thoughtfully, and perhaps decide it wasn't worth a fight in front of Mrs Cartwright. She grabbed her pencil case and sat down next to him—but she moved the chair further away first, as though he smelled.

Mrs Cartwright handed out a worksheet about Roman gladiators and beast fights, and Alfie enjoyed himself filling in the answers from that bit of the film, imagining Grace as a criminal thrown to the wild beasts. Penguin would enjoy being a ferocious panther, he thought.

The second side of the sheet had to be done with a partner. Alfie sighed and glanced up to see if Grace was ready, and found she was staring at him, looking equally unkeen.

'We have to write a play,' he muttered.

'Mmm.'

'You any good at writing?'

She shrugged. 'We can have two characters. Then I'll write one and you do one.'

Alfie nodded. It seemed the easiest way. 'I'm going to be one of those ones with a net and the thing like a garden fork,' he added quickly.

Grace shrugged. 'OK, but you'll lose. I'll be the one with the helmet and all the armour.'

Alfie nibbled his pencil, wondering if she was right. 'All that armour's heavy,' he pointed out. 'You won't be able to catch me. It's weird that they knew each other, isn't it? They probably had breakfast and talked about who was going to win.'

Grace nodded, looking interested. 'Maybe that's what we should do— our gladiators could be friends having breakfast at the gladiator training camp, and then they find out they have to fight each other.'

'What did Romans eat for

breakfast?' Alfie asked.

'Just bread, Alfie,' Mrs Cartwright said over his shoulder. 'Sounds like you two are doing really well. Keep going!'

Alfie blinked, surprised to find that he was actually enjoying himself. 'We could finish it off after school if you want,' he suggested hesitantly to Grace, when Mrs Cartwright told them it was time to stop.

Grace smiled, a real smile, not the sort of horrible smirk he thought of her making. 'Can I come to yours? Penguin would come and sit with us, wouldn't he?'

Alfie stared at her. 'Isn't he at your house?'

Grace shook her head. 'Not for ages. Days and days.'

Alfie frowned. He didn't understand. Penguin was at Grace's house, Alfie knew he was. Because he certainly wasn't at Alfie's. 'I haven't seen him since Saturday afternoon.' He dropped his voice to a whisper—it felt like some terrible secret. 'I thought he'd gone back to yours! He has to be there . . .'

Grace looked worried. 'He only ever

stayed that one night. Then he popped in every so often. And then he had the last of the bag of cat treats, and I don't think toast crusts were good enough. He gave me a sort of look when I offered him one.'

'He only likes them with Marmite on,' Alfie murmured. 'But if he's not at yours, where's he gone?'

Grace was frowning. 'He couldn't have another house, could he?'

'I don't think so.' Alfie looked doubtful. 'Not unless he was only there when I was at school. He never went anywhere else until you turned up,' he added. All those thoughts about run-over cats he'd had when Penguin disappeared the previous weekend were flooding back. 'What if he's been hit by a car?' he muttered shakily, quite forgetting to blame Grace.

'Someone would have told you. He's got a tag on his collar, hasn't he?' Grace pointed out.

'I suppose.' Alfie nodded, suddenly grateful for the collar. 'But—where is he then?'

'Maybe he's got shut in somewhere.

Look, I'll ask my mum, she's picking me up. We can go and look for him together.'

*   *   *

But when they dashed across the playground together, leaving Oliver standing gaping at the classroom door, only Alfie's mum was there waving at them.

Grace slowed up, frowning and peering through the fence for her mum.

'Grace, your mum asked me to fetch you,' Alfie's mum called quietly, and Grace slouched over to her, looking reluctant.

'Is something wrong?' she asked. She looked grumpy, but Alfie realized it was because she was frightened.

Alfie's mum nibbled her bottom lip and nodded. 'She was really sorry, Grace. She didn't want you to be upset, but it was all a bit of a rush. Your gran's not very well, you see.'

Grace glared at her. 'I know that! She hasn't been well for ages. That's why we came.'

'Ye-es, but she's had to go into hospital. It happened at lunch time,' Mum explained. 'Your mum's with her; that's why she asked me to pick you up.'

'When will they be back?' Grace asked. Her water bottle rolled out of her fingers, and Alfie picked it up for her.

Alfie's mum shook her head. 'Your mum really wasn't sure. She didn't know exactly what was wrong with your gran, and she wants to stay at the hospital while they find out, you see.' She smiled at Grace. 'We arranged that you can stay with us if she's got to be there overnight.'

Grace took her water bottle back from Alfie. Her fingers felt cold when he touched them, by accident. 'All right,' she whispered, even though Alfie didn't think she had much choice.

6

Grace trailed along behind Alfie and his mum. Alfie kept glancing back at her, not sure what to say. He'd have been upset if it was either of his grandmas in hospital. Grace actually lived with her gran, so it must be even worse.

He hung back to walk next to her, and she slowed down to pigeon steps, and then reluctantly caught up with him. 'What?' she muttered ungraciously.

'Um. You still want to go and look for Penguin?' he asked. He felt bad saying it, but Penguin was still missing, even if Grace's gran was in hospital.

Grace sighed, a very tiny sigh, and nodded.

'OK. Um, don't tell my mum? She'll want to come with us, and I bet we can look better if we just sneak around—most of the gardens have got holes in the fences, like ours does. I've watched Penguin going off exploring.'

'From in my tree, I bet!' Grace's eyes sparkled, but she seemed glad to be almost-cross. Alfie just shrugged and grinned at her. She elbowed him, and he elbowed her back, in a friendly sort of way.

'What shall we have for tea?' Alfie's mum asked, looking back from the pushchair. Alfie jumped away from Grace and tried to look as though he hadn't been pushing.

'Lasagne!' Grace suggested promptly. 'Takes ages to make!' she whispered to Alfie, when he looked at her in surprise. 'We want her busy, don't we?'

'Er, really?' Alfie's mum murmured, looking a little shocked. 'Well, I was thinking more along the lines of sausages, but I suppose . . .'

Behind his mum's back, Alfie beamed at Grace and flashed a sly thumbs up. She nodded regally. She was clearly a mistress of deception.

Alfie was impressed.

Once they got home, Alfie and Grace disappeared into the garden, promising to be back in for tea.

'Is it OK if we climb over the fence into my garden too?' Grace asked very politely. 'I'd like to show Alfie my den.'

'Well, as long as you're careful,' Alfie's mum agreed.

'Now if she can't see us she'll just think we're in my garden,' Grace whispered conspiratorially as they headed down to the end of the garden. 'And I didn't tell her about the loose board, either. Where shall we look first? I'm sure he isn't anywhere round my house, honestly.'

Alfie nodded. 'He goes under our back fence sometimes. That's the Morrises' garden, and they're not usually in until later. We could go and check there. Then there's the little copse behind your garden that's full of holes and stuff. And he likes the allotments on the corner. That's a couple more gardens away, but if we were sneaky going along the back fences, I bet no one would see us.'

Grace nodded, not looking the slightest bit daunted by all this skulduggery. Alfie decided he almost liked her, even if she was a thieving cat-rustler.

He led her down to the back fence of his garden, helpfully hidden behind a screen of sweet pea poles, and pointed out the rather dank hole under the fence. It was definitely more cat-sized than Alfie-and-Grace-sized, but then Penguin was a large cat, and they were both reasonably skinny.

Grace eyed it doubtfully, and then looked him up and down. 'You first.'

Alfie took a deep breath in and lay down, ready to squirm.

'Do you want me to push you?' Grace asked helpfully, squatting down by his middle.

'No!' Alfie retorted from the other side of the fence. 'I can do it with my elbows. Ow, I'm through. Your turn!'

Grace wriggled daintily through the hole, the only casualty her bunches, which were decidedly uneven when she stood up with Alfie on the other side of the fence. She straightened them thoughtfully as they peered round the bush they'd emerged into and along the Morrises' garden. 'They're definitely out?'

Alfie shrugged. 'Neither of them gets home till about six.'

Grace smiled at him. 'You really did spy out of that tree, didn't you? Do you know what everybody does round here?'

Alfie ducked his head, flushing. 'It's good for spotting stuff, that's all. I miss it,' he added in a mutter.

Grace nodded. 'You can maybe borrow it sometimes. Should we call for Penguin, do you think? Or is here too close? Wouldn't you have heard him meowing if he was stuck somewhere so near?'

Alfie crouched down and peered right under the bush. 'I guess so. And they don't have a shed for him to be shut in or anything like that. Penguin!' he called quietly just in case. 'Penguin!'

There was no answering mew, and he stood up, shaking his head. 'Let's go next door. Then we're on the way to the allotments. And the people next door but one have got a shed. It's worth a look.'

The Morrises' side fence was worryingly solid, with no useful loose boards or holes underneath. But they did have a small plum tree that Alfie could shove Grace into, and she could haul him up after her. Then they sat there, wobbling, and peering down into the little wooded patch on the other side of the fence. It was a sort of tiny nature reserve that belonged to the council, with a pond in it that school took them to every so often to do pond dipping. Pond dipping was mostly just an excuse for flicking slime at the girls, as far as Alfie and Oliver and most of their friends were concerned. Last time Asha had shoved Oliver back when he put something disgusting down her wellies, and he'd actually fallen in the pond. Year Two (they'd been Year Two then) had been banned from pond dipping after that.

Alfie frowned down at the ground, which seemed a long way away. 'I think we just have to jump.'

Grace nodded. 'Those ferny things

look quite soft.'

'They're nettles,' Alfie told her, leaning down for a closer look.

'No! This bit.'

'Oh. OK, yeah. Maybe. Shall I jump then?'

Grace nodded, and settled herself in the tree as though she was preparing to watch something funny.

It actually wasn't that far down, and Alfie almost missed the nettles. Not quite, but almost. He sucked his hand. 'Aim this way,' he pointed, looking up at Grace in the tree.

Grace edged out away from the tree and perched herself on the edge of the fence, holding on to a branch. Then she jumped with a yell, landing spreadeagled in the middle of the ferns and gasping with laughter.

'Are you all right?' Alfie asked, helping her up. But she was all right enough to be giggling, too much to say anything.

'Your dress is covered in stuff,' he told her, but Grace only shrugged. She took a deep, shaky breath, and sighed.

'That was funny.'

'Are you really all right?' Alfie eyed her doubtfully. 'You look sort of weird.'

Grace nodded, and stopped looking at him. 'I just want to find Penguin,' she muttered. 'I can do something about that. I can't help Gran.'

'Is she really ill?' Alfie asked.

Grace nodded. 'She has been for ages, I think. We didn't know. Mum had a massive row with her years ago. I've hardly even met her before. She sent presents, really nice ones. And she'd phone at Christmas and stuff, but I never knew what to say. Last time she phoned she told Mum how ill she was, and Mum came to see her. Then she came back and told me we were moving!'

Alfie shook his head. 'Just like that?'

Grace nodded bitterly. 'Right at the end of the summer holidays. I didn't even get to start the new term or say goodbye at school. Only to my two best friends.'

Alfie swallowed. He couldn't imagine it. 'Let's go this way,' he muttered, pulling her arm gently. 'Are

73

you staying?' he asked, as they set off, wading through the bracken.

Grace shrugged. 'Mum says so. But, if Gran's really ill—really badly ill, I mean . . .' She trailed off.

'Mm. You could go home again.' Alfie flushed scarlet as soon as he said it, wishing he hadn't.

Grace nodded. 'It's really bad that I think that, isn't it?' she asked miserably.

'I don't think it is.' Alfie looked back at her as she tracked him through the waist-high leaves. 'You've only known her about a week, haven't you?'

Grace nodded. 'But she is my grandma,' she pointed out. 'I feel horrible that I'm more worried about your cat than her.'

Alfie shrugged. 'Well, it's like you said. You can't do anything about her, but you can help me find Penguin. Once we've found him, I'll help you worry about her, if you like.'

Grace smiled. 'All right. We should call him.'

They called and called. There were strange rustles, and leaves shook here and there, but it was only birds, and a dirty, skinny fox that shot across the faint path in front of them and made Grace shriek.

Alfie patted her. 'You don't need to be scared of them. They're a pain, Mum says. They just tip the bins over and eat the rubbish.' But his heart was thumping fast too.

'Gran likes them,' Grace said, her voice still a little shaky with surprise. 'She knows loads about animals, really funny things sometimes. Foxes used to hide out in her garden. One of her notes said so. She leaves notes for herself everywhere,' she added. 'She says her memory's going and she doesn't want to forget anything. She's got notebooks in every room, and little sticky notes all over the place. It's weird.' She paused for a minute, as though she wasn't sure whether or not to go on. Then she started again all in a rush. 'Lots of them are about me. She's written my name inside the front cover of all the books, so she doesn't forget what it is.'

'Oh.' Alfie nodded, not sure what

to say. 'She still calls me Lucy a lot, though. That's my mum's name.' She looked around, shaking her head as if she didn't want to think about it any more. 'He isn't here, is he? Where shall we go now?'

Alfie looked thoughtfully through the trees. 'The allotments. I reckon he goes there for bits of people's sandwiches. He could have got shut in somewhere.' He carefully didn't mention the road between the wood and the allotments. That was something he didn't want to think about.

Grace looked at it as they came out of the little gate, but she didn't say anything either. They just waited, looking carefully both ways. Alfie wasn't allowed to cross roads on his own, and he suspected Grace wasn't either. But they'd broken enough rules that afternoon not to care.

The allotments weren't that busy on a weekday afternoon—most people had gone home to think about dinner, Alfie guessed, inwardly thanking Grace for her sneaky lasagne plan. He hoped

Mum hadn't spotted they'd gone yet. If they didn't find Penguin soon they'd have to go back, but they could go the street way, which would be quicker, and sneak back down the side path so Mum didn't notice.

'Lots of sheds,' Grace said thoughtfully, looking around the tidy little plots.

Alfie nodded. 'And I bet they're all locked. We'll just have to shout for him, see what happens.'

Treading cautiously around a row of tall green things—he had no idea what they were—Alfie pressed his nose up against the window of a small, slightly tumbledown shed and peered in. All he could see were greyish, shadowy shapes. He banged on the glass. 'Penguin? Penguin!'

He was sure Penguin would have answered if he'd been there. All that happened was an old lady digging on another plot looked round at them. Alfie sighed. He'd been really hoping. But it was silly to think that Penguin would be in the very first shed. They couldn't just give up.

'She's going to come and tell us off in a minute,' Grace predicted. 'Let's go

and look at some more. Quickly!'

The shed on the next plot was even more battered. The roof was half covered in a green tarpaulin where the proper roofing had worn away, and there were boards half hanging off in places. Alfie felt a little less anxious going up to this one—it didn't look as though anyone was going to complain about him damaging it. He put his hands up against the glass, which was striped with Sellotape,

and called, 'Penguin?' as he peered in.

There was a scuffling noise, and then a frantic mew—frantic, but tired, as though the cat inside had been calling for ages, and had given up.

Grace ran up next to him, jumping over a row of flowers. 'It's him! You found him, Alfie!'

Alfie hugged her, without actually meaning to. 'He sounds all right, doesn't he? Not hurt or anything? I can't see him!'

Grace looked along the shed to the door. 'And we can't get in. It's locked.'

'What are you children doing?'

Alfie yelped and jumped round. It was the old lady who'd been watching them. She looked rather annoyed. 'It's my cat . . .' he whispered. 'He's been lost. He's shut in this shed. We came looking for him, that's all.'

'You shouldn't be poking around the allotments,' the old lady said firmly.

'He's been missing for two whole nights,' Grace said pleadingly. 'He could have been shut in here all that time. We're only trying to get him back, we're not hurting anything.'

'You're standing on a row of winter cabbages!' the old lady snapped, and Grace jumped back against the shed. 'But if there really is a cat in there, we shall certainly have to get him out. The problem is that that's Joe Orton's shed, and he's on holiday this week.'

Alfie swallowed back sudden tears, looking at the padlock on the door. Was Penguin going to have stay in there for the rest of the week? He supposed they could poke food through the little holes . . . 'It's all right, Penguin,' he murmured. 'We'll do something . . .'

There was only a very small meow in response.

'Don't worry.' The old lady seemed to have decided she was on their side since Grace jumped off the cabbages. 'The allotment committee keeps telling Joe he needs to sort out this shed, but for once it's a blessing. The roof's half gone. Huge hole in it. It might well be how your cat got in there in the first place.'

'I could climb up there,' Grace said, looking at the water butt. 'Or I could if you pushed me, Alfie.'

'You won't be able to get out again.' Alfie shook his head. 'Then you and Penguin would both be stuck in there. I suppose at least it would cheer him up. But your mum would kill mine if she came back home and Mum said you were stuck in a shed.'

'Joe's got a stepladder in there that he uses for pruning his apple tree,' the old lady said thoughtfully. 'You should be able to use that to get out.'

'Alfie, crouch down so I can climb on your back,' Grace ordered.

Alfie did as he was told. Since he'd heard Penguin mewing, he was so happy he didn't mind Grace bossing him around. 'Ow, you're so heavy!' he yelped, as she half-jumped off his back on to the top of the water butt, which thankfully still had its lid.

He straightened up and watched anxiously as she pulled the tarpaulin aside and peered into the hole.

'Is he all right?'

'I think so—he's walking round and round in circles,' she reported back. 'He's not limping or anything. Hi,

Penguin! We're going to get you out!'

'Can you get down in there safely?' the old lady called.

'There's a wheelbarrow,' Grace told her, swinging one leg into the hole, and then the other. Alfie clutched the rim of the water butt nervously as he watched her jump. He should have climbed up really. After all, Penguin was his cat. Alfie hadn't realized how brave Grace was. He was suddenly glad she'd come searching with him.

There was a loud clanging as Grace hit the wheelbarrow, and an anxious hiss from Penguin.

'Are you all right?' Alfie yelled.

Grace's voice came back echoey but somehow muffled.

'Yes. Ow. I've got splinters, but I'm all right. Penguin's sulking; he didn't like the bang. I'm getting the stepladder.'

There was a series of scraping and scuffling sounds, and then an angry yowl, followed by some muttering, which Alfie thought sounded like, Stupid ungrateful cat. Then Penguin's front paws, very stiff and cross,

83

appeared out of the hole in the roof, quickly followed by the rest of him, and by Grace, looking scratched but pleased with herself.

Penguin saw Alfie and skidded out of Grace's arms and down the roof with a joyful yowl. Alfie caught him laughing, and hugged him.

'You've got thinner.' He grinned. 'The vet'll be pleased.'

Penguin put one paw on each of Alfie's shoulders, as though he was trying to hug him back, and purred like a lawnmower.

'Do you need help?' Alfie called up, suddenly remembering Grace, but she was already half out of the hole, wriggling back to the water butt.

'He isn't the slightest bit thankful!' she told Alfie as she slid down the side. 'Look, he scratched me all over!'

'He was scared,' Alfie said apologetically, hugging Penguin even tighter. He didn't even care if Penguin wanted to go to Grace's house sometimes, he realized. As long as he knew he'd come back.

7

Alfie turned over in his sleep, reaching out automatically to cuddle Penguin close. He startled awake when his hand stroked the cold paint of the wall. Penguin had gone again!

'It's all right, he's here.'

Alfie sat up, shaking his head blearily. The room was quite dark, just a little moonlight coming through his curtains, and for a moment he couldn't imagine who it was speaking to him. He blinked and narrowed his eyes at the figure in the window. Then he remembered—Grace. She had been on his ready bed on the floor—he had offered her the real bed, as Mum had said he ought to, but she said she didn't mind.

'What are you doing?' he asked sleepily. 'What time is it?'

then took a deep breath and started again. 'You rescued him; that makes you his part-owner. I don't mind if he goes to your house sometimes. I don't mind much, anyway.'

Grace didn't say anything.

'If you do have to move, he'll still be partly yours. I'll send you pictures.'

She laughed. 'He could come and visit me on the train. You could tie his ticket on his collar. I read about a cat that did that on buses. I bet he could.' She was quiet for a minute. 'Thanks, Alfie. You can have half shares in the tree, if you like.' Then she sniggered. 'Yeah, you can have the top branches . . .'

Alfie snorted.

Grace sighed again. 'I hope we don't go.'

'I'll buy him a season ticket for the train . . .' Alfie murmured sleepily. 'Go back to bed, Grace.'

But he didn't think she moved. As he settled back to sleep, he could still see her, curled up against the window glass, Penguin's ears pricked up in little dark triangles against the moonlight.

'Your gran won't mind?' Alfie asked cautiously, following Grace through her front door.

'No. She was nice about school. She kept asking if I'd made any friends. She was worried about me. She said to bring someone home for tea.'

'Yeah, but I think she meant when she was here,' Alfie muttered as he followed her into the kitchen. Grace's mum was still at the hospital, where her gran was apparently getting much better. She'd been back to talk to Grace that morning before school, and Alfie's mum had told her that Grace had been an angel.

Alfie had nearly laughed out loud, and Grace had been biting her lip. His mum still thought they'd been in Grace's garden the whole time. They'd sneaked back in round the side path, while his mum was wrestling with sheets of dried pasta. Alfie hadn't liked the lasagne, but Grace had had loads, and told his mum it was brilliant. Alfie

88

had fed a lot of his to Penguin, who definitely needed to catch up after that many missed meals. He knew he shouldn't be doing it, but just thinking of Penguin shut up and miserable in the shed made it impossible not to.

'Wow, I see what you mean about the notes,' Alfie said, staring around at the cupboards. They were all covered in them, little sticky notes, all colours and shapes, with spiky, scratchy writing all over them.

'Weird, isn't it?' Grace sighed. 'They're about all sorts of stuff. When to pay the milkman. People's birthdays. That kind of thing. She's really scared about forgetting something important.'

Alfie nodded. There were even sticky notes on the kitchen window, and he leaned forward to read one. 'What's a nuthatch?' he asked Grace.

'Oh, it's a bird. She loves watching the birds. She has all those feeders hanging off the hooks outside the window. She was telling Mum, that's what made her realize she was getting worse—she couldn't get out of the back door to go and fill them up. I heard her, on the phone. She was crying. That's when Mum said she had to come and see her.' Grace picked up a leather case from by the kettle. 'Look, these are her binoculars. They're really good ones. She could see right down to the end of the garden.' She opened the case and handed the heavy black binoculars to Alfie. 'See?'

Alfie held them up to his eyes, frowning as he tried to make them focus. Then he gulped, realizing what the strange brownish lines were. Branches. A few leaves had fallen from the old apple tree already, and the lower branches were dark and spidery.

'She could see the tree,' he muttered.

Grace nodded. 'Oh yes. Further than that, probably.'

'But then she could see me, all the time!' Alfie told her, his voice gone high with panic. 'She knew I was in her garden!'

Grace smiled. 'Who do you think put the rope there, silly? Look.' She pointed to another of the notes on the window, a blue cloud-shaped one, faded and curled at the edges.

Remember to get rope out of garage for that boy.

'She was a lot better then, of course,' Grace added.

Alfie nodded silently. He still couldn't believe she'd known. He smiled to himself. He'd been thinking Mrs Barratt was a witch all this time, but really she was more like a fairy godmother.

'Perhaps a bunch of flowers?' Alfie's mum suggested.

Alfie shook his head. 'No. That's really boring. I want to get Mrs Barratt something special.'

His mum frowned. 'Yes, I know. I just can't think what, though. Why does it matter so much?'

'I just do . . .' Alfie muttered. 'It's important. She—er—she's nice about Penguin, even though he chases the birds in her garden, Grace said so. And there was a note in her kitchen about it. She was going to ask one of her friends from the Over Sixties to buy her a water pistol to try and put him off, instead of complaining about him.'

'I'm still not sure about you and Grace going round there without

Grace's mum or her gran,' Mum murmured worriedly.

'We're helping!' Alfie told her indignantly. 'We refilled all the bird feeders. Maybe I could buy her a new one of those? They've got them in the pet shop.'

His dad glanced up, smiling. 'I think the seven she's got might be enough already, Alfie. If you want to do something to help her, why don't you get a bell for Penguin's collar? Then he couldn't chase the birds, could he?'

Alfie nodded. 'Can we go now? To the pet shop? Grace said her mum was bringing her gran home later today.' He was standing right next to his dad, bouncing slightly with eagerness.

His dad sighed, and yawned. He'd been on shift and had just got home. 'Shouldn't have said it, should I? Come on, then.'

'I'll just get my pocket money!'

*   *   *

Alfie shuffled nervously into Grace's

kitchen, which was large enough for an armchair in the corner, set just where Mrs Barratt could see the birds at the window feeders. Even though the old lady had known he was in her garden all along and hadn't ever said anything—even all those times his mum had stopped to chat with her!— he still felt funny about meeting her for real. He didn't even know what she looked like.

She was sitting in the armchair, and his first thought was that she looked like a little bird herself. She had the most enormous beak-like nose, and he couldn't tear his eyes away from it. It was quite like Grace's, he realized, except that the rest of Mrs Barratt's face seemed to have sunken away, leaving the nose to be what one noticed first.

'This is my gran,' Grace said, pulling him forward. Her mum was hovering around anxiously, making tea, but really watching Mrs Barratt with worried eyes. 'Gran, this is Alfie, you know, from next door?'

'Alfie . . .' Mrs Barratt frowned. 'Oh

dear. I'm sure your mother did tell me that, but I could never remember. But your beautiful cat is called Penguin, isn't he?'

Alfie nodded shyly.

'Such a good name—I don't forget that one. It suits him perfectly.'

'It does!' Alfie looked delighted. Most people frowned when he told them Penguin's name, or at least laughed as if they thought it was stupid. He smiled at Mrs Barratt. 'I've brought you a present. You can open it, but then I have to take it back to mine . . . You'll see when you open it.' He thrust the tiny parcel at her, feeling embarrassed.

Mrs Barratt peered down at it, smiling. 'Open it for me, dear. Useless old fingers.'

Carefully, Alfie undid the tape, and slid off the ribbon Mum had found for him. Then he put the open parcel on the arm of the chair for her to see. 'Dad said just one, but I thought three would be better. Penguin's a big cat.'

The bells shone and glittered as

95

Mrs Barratt stared down at them, and laughed. 'Poor Penguin. Well, with three bells, there'll be no keeping his whereabouts a secret.'

Grace crouched down next to her. 'You knew I'd brought him in? I thought no one saw him!'

Mrs Barratt laughed. 'There's a lot of him to hide, Lucy. Oh dear—Grace, I mean. I don't mind if Alfie doesn't.'

'I've given her half of him,' Alfie muttered. 'Penguin likes her, even though it's mostly because she buys him those expensive fishy cat treats. And she helped me rescue him out of a shed on the allotments last week.'

'Clever girl . . .' Mrs Barratt sounded weary, and Alfie stepped back, looking anxiously up at Grace's mother. But the old lady went on. 'You'll have to stay then, Lucy, won't you, if you have a cat . . .'

Alfie glanced between Grace and her mother. Which of them was Mrs Barratt talking to? Or perhaps she meant to say it to both of them.

Grace's mother sighed, but she was smiling. She put a cup of tea on the little table next to Mrs Barratt's chair. 'We talked about it, Grace, in the hospital. While Gran was getting better. She needs us to stay. I know you want to go back home, but she needs us here. We can visit your friends . . .'

'But I want to stay here!' Grace nearly tipped the tea over, leaping up to grab her mother. 'I thought we'd have to go. Alfie was going to put Penguin on the train for me!'

There was a sudden scuffling from outside the window, and they all jumped. A moon-shaped black and white face was peering curiously through the glass, bird feeders swinging above him.

'If you're going to share him,' Mrs Barratt said faintly, 'you'd better make sure you know who's feeding him when. If that cat gets any bigger, he won't be able to move, let alone chase birds.'

Alfie nodded. 'We will. We can shout over the fence.'

Grace's mother opened the kitchen window, and Penguin stepped delicately over the sill and sat down on the counter, staring smugly round at them all.

Alfie scratched him under the chin, and Grace tickled behind his neat ears. Penguin's whiskers twitched happily. He was quite convinced he could find a way to get at least three breakfasts.

Look after your cat.

Penguin is a lovely cat, but he is overweight. While this might look cuddly, it isn't good for him and could lead to him getting poorly. Here's how to help your own cat get into shape.

1. Make sure you play with your cat every day. Chasing balls and pouncing on strings is great exercise and will keep your cat active and happy. It is great fun for you, too.

2. Make sure your cat has a scratching post or climbing tower to keep them busy and active while you are at school.

3. Make mealtimes more challenging. Place your feline's favourite food at the top of their climbing tower or at the top of the stairs. This will make your cat work a little bit harder for their supper.

4. Cut down on the number of treats and snacks between your moggy's mealtimes. This may feel mean, but take the time to stroke or groom your cat instead so that they know you love them.

If you are worried about your cat's weight, ask your parents to take them to the vet. Your vet will be able to advise you on anything else you could do to keep your precious pet fit and healthy.